WITHDRAWN

WOW!
NEW
YORK
CITY

For New York City, we will always miss you.
—Puck

Con cariño para mi esposa Diana Elizabeth y mis hijos Dariana y Mateo
—Rey David Rojas

GREAT CITY BOOKS™

WOW!
NEW
YORK
CITY

By Puck
Art by Rey David Rojas

duopress
New York

Can you build a city with a paper clip?

Let's use our imagination...

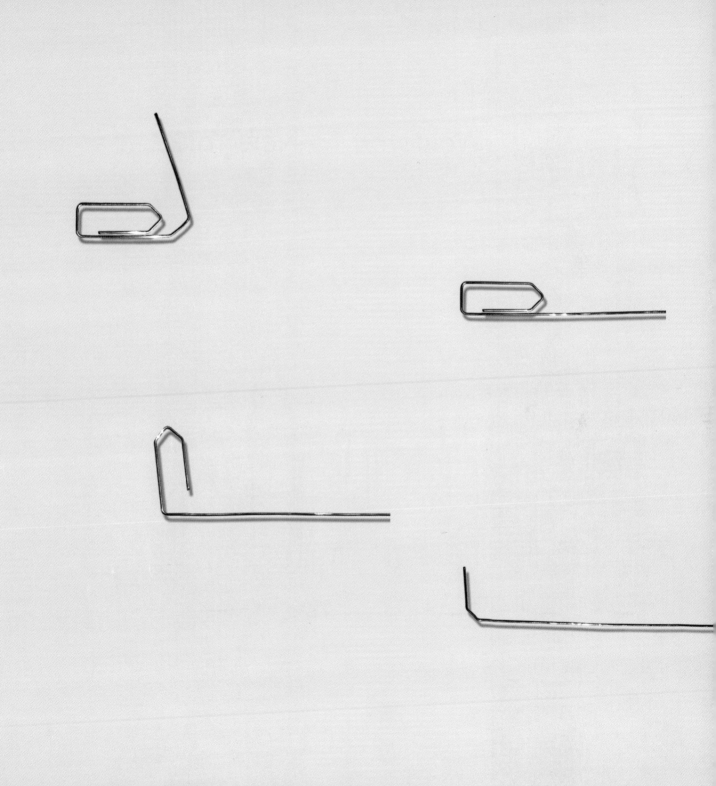

Welcome to New York,

the BIG APPLE!

Hop in a taxi!
We're going on a tour.

First stop:
the Empire State Building.

Let's go to the top!

Wow! Look at this!

You can see the Chrysler Building.

Now let's walk and find something to eat. It's safe to cross!

Look, a fire truck!
Cool!

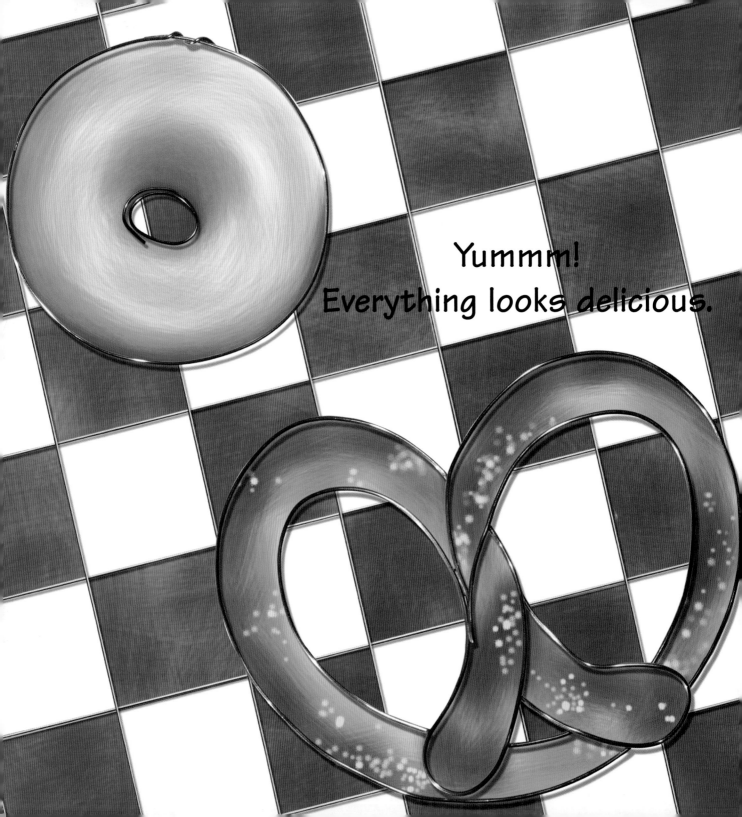

Yummm!
Everything looks delicious.

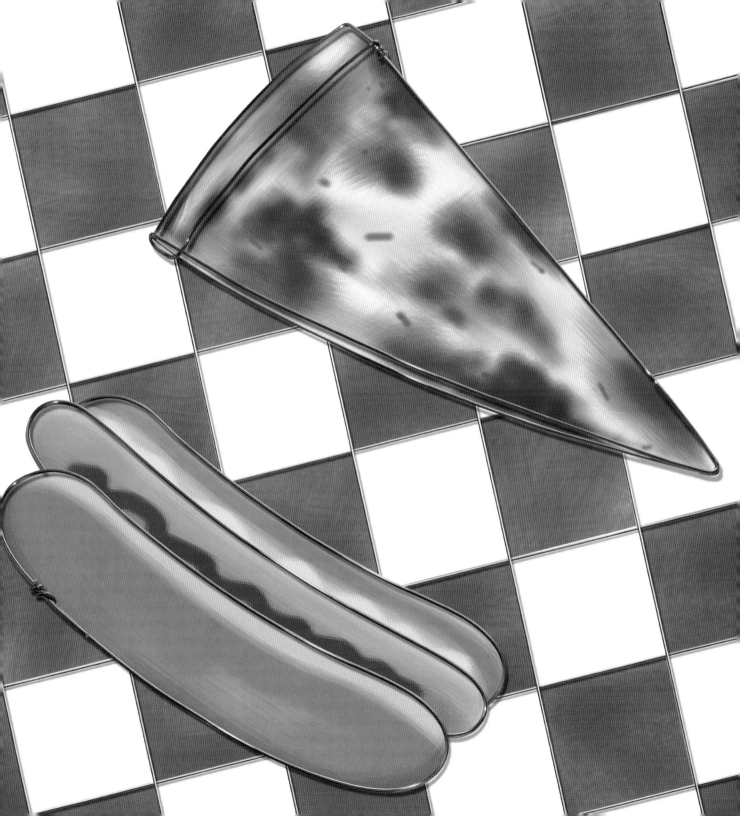

How about a rest?
Central Park is the perfect place to sit and relax.

Ok, we're ready to go again.
There is one friend we must visit.

Let's take the ferry!

Hello, Lady Liberty!

Now, where shall we go to end our day?

Let's get on the subway and head to . . .

. . . the Brooklyn Bridge!

Thank you for a wonderful day, New York!

New York Taxis

Raise your arm and hail a cab! A New York taxi is on its way. But there is a trick you should know if you want the cab to stop. Look at the lights on top of the cab. When just the medallion number—the combination of numbers and letters in the center—is lit, the cab is available. When the side lamps are lit, the cab is off-duty. When no lights are lit, the cab already has a passenger.

In Case You Wonder: More than 12,000 taxis cruise the city every day. All of them are yellow.

Pretzels

Every day is pretzel day in New York. Try one from a street cart in Central Park or at one of the many New York sports stadiums.

The Statue of Liberty

Say hello to a very special lady: the Statue of Liberty. This magnificent monument was a gift from France to the United States to celebrate the one-hundred-year anniversary of the signing of our Declaration of Independence in 1886. Today, the Lady of the Harbor is the most recognized symbol in the United States and a favorite place for New Yorkers and visitors.

French artist Frédéric Auguste Bartholdi modeled the copper sculpture after his mother, Charlotte, with the help of Maurice Koechlin, the chief designer of another international icon—the Eiffel Tower in Paris, France. The statue is 151 feet tall, but with the pedestal and foundation, it reaches 305 feet. The face alone measures more than 8 feet tall with a nose 4 feet and 6 inches high!

In Case You Wonder: The official name of the Statue of Liberty is Liberty Enlightening the World (English for La liberté éclairant le monde)

The Big Apple

Walk to the corner of West 54th Street & Broadway and you will find a street sign that reads "Big Apple Corner." Cool, right? You are in the core of the apple. But why is New York called the Big Apple, anyway? Well, as the story goes, John J. Fitz Gerald, a sportswriter for the *New York Morning Telegraph*, first used the phrase in the 1920s when talking about the horse racing courses in New York and their big prizes. In the 1930s, New York became the jazz capital of the world, and jazz musicians started calling the city the Big Apple because, as they said, "There are many apples on the tree, but only one Big Apple: New York City."

And why is the corner of 54th & Broadway called "Big Apple Corner"? Well, that's because John J. Fitz Gerald lived there for 30 years.

Fire Truck

Meet New York's Bravest, the New York City firefighters. With more than 11,000 uniformed officers and firefighters, the Fire Department of New York (FDNY) is the largest municipal fire department in the United States. As you can imagine, protecting a city like New York is a big challenge, but the FDNY is always ready to take care of all the high-rise buildings, bridges, tunnels, and the occasional cat climbing up a tree. If you want to see and know more about these city heroes you can go to the New York City Fire Museum, located in a renovated 1904 firehouse at 278 Spring Street in SoHo.

In Case You Wonder: The FDNY attends 500,000 emergency calls a year!

The Empire State Building

(350 Fifth Avenue, between 33rd and 34th Streets)

Do you feel like climbing 1860 steps and 102 floors to reach the top of the Empire State Building? Well, you don't really have to. The tallest building in New York has 73 elevators that will take you from the lobby to the 86th floor in less than one minute.

The Empire State is an old pal. It was constructed between 1929 and 1931, and it has a total height of 1,454 feet to the top of the lightning rod. By the way, this lightning rod is always busy as it gets struck by lightning around 100 times each year!

In Case You Wonder: The Empire State has 6,500 windows.

Empire State Observation Decks

Take a look—King Kong Style! In the movie *King Kong*, we saw the gigantic ape climbing the Empire State Building to try to do some not-very-nice things. But you can climb to one of the two observatories and take a really nice look at the city and beyond. The lower deck on the 86th floor is 1,050 feet from the ground, and the one on the 102nd floor is 1,224 feet up. On a clear day you can see as far as 80 miles—well into New Jersey! The observation decks are open every day from 8:00 a.m. to 2:00 a.m.

Hot Dog

Hot dogs were not invented in New York, but history tells us that it was a New Yorker who used this quirky name for a sausage in a bun for the first time more than a hundred years ago. In any case, hot dogs are the kings of the New York corners.

Chrysler Building

(405 Lexington Avenue, corner of 42nd Street)

The Chrysler Building may have been the world's tallest building for only 11 months before it was surpassed by the Empire State Building in 1931, but most people agree that this is one of the most gorgeous buildings in the world. With a total height of 1,407 feet, this is a chic construction incorporating many elements that were used on Chrysler cars at the time. The corners of 61st floor have replicas of the beautiful eagles on the 1929 Chrysler cars, and the decorations on the 31st floor corners are replicas of Chrysler radiator caps.

The silver crown, the most famous element on the building, was built with a special steel that not only doesn't rust, but shines like nothing else in the Big Apple.

In Case You Wonder:
The Chrysler Building has 3,826,000 bricks.

New York–style Pizza

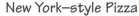

Get a plain slice from that pie! If you want pizza in New York, you need to know a few important things. 1) New York-style pizza is thin, and slices should be foldable. 2) Traditional toppings are mozzarella cheese and tomato sauce. We call that "plain." 3) Every New Yorker has a favorite pizza place, and the top three are (arguably) Lombardi's, Grimaldi's, and John's. What's your favorite?

New York City Subway

From New York to Chicago. This is how far the New York subway would take you if you laid out the 660 miles of track that this system uses to move millions of people around the city every day. How many people? Well, a lot! The New York subway delivers an average of five million trips on weekdays. To move so many people, this rapid system needs a lot of subway cars (more than 6,400!), plenty of stations (468!), and no closing hours (the subway runs 24 hours a day, 365 days a year). If New York is the city that never sleeps, it certainly helps to have this tireless subway system.

Staten Island Ferry

All aboard! The ferry is leaving the dock, and one of the best-kept secrets in New York is about to start a journey between Manhattan and Staten Island. The trip is smooth and the sights are awesome: lower Manhattan and the Brooklyn Bridge to the north, the Statue of Liberty, Ellis Island, and New Jersey to the west, Governors Island and Brooklyn to the east, and Staten Island and the Verrazano Bridge to the south.

This 5.2-mile trip from lower Manhattan to Staten Island takes 25 minutes, it runs 24 hours a day, and it is free! The Staten Island Ferry is more than a fun way to see the city; 65,000 people take the trip to commute from home to work and back every weekday.

In Case You Wonder: Staten Island is one of the five boroughs in New York City. The other boroughs are Brooklyn, the Bronx, Queens, and Manhattan.

The Brooklyn Bridge

By foot, bike, or car, crossing the Brooklyn Bridge is one of the greatest New York experiences. This massive bridge, one of the oldest suspension bridges in the world, stretches 5,989 feet over the East River to connect Manhattan and Brooklyn. When the bridge opened in 1883, it was the first steel-wire suspension bridge on the planet, using approximately 3,600 miles of wire.

If you cross the Brooklyn Bridge by foot, stop in the two towers (276.5 feet tall) where you can read the history of this fantastic bridge while enjoing breathtaking views of Manhattan and Brooklyn.

In Case You Wonder: One week after its opening, on May 30, 1883, a rumor that the bridge was going to collapse caused a tragic stampede. To demonstrate its stability, circus owner P. T. Barnum led a parade of 21 elephants over the bridge.

Bagels

Doughy, chewy, toasted, not toasted, with or without cream cheese and lox, plain, onion, garlic, sesame, poppy, or "everything," New York City bagels are as famous as the Empire State Building. A bagel in New York is like nothing else.

Central Park

Every New Yorker has a favorite spot in Central Park. What's yours? Is it one of the 8,968 benches or one of the 26,000 trees? How about hiding under a bridge or climbing, running, swinging, and splashing, in one of the 37 playgrounds in the park? Of course, the Central Park Zoo is a big favorite and so are the two ice-skating rinks (in the summer, one of the ice rinks is a swimming pool). Or perhaps the carousel, or the Alice in Wonderland sculpture, or rowboating on the lake? With so many things to do, Central Park is an exciting place. But you can always lie down in the grass and look at the blue sky.

On the West Side of Central Park, between 71st and 74th Streets, you'll find Strawberry Fields. This area and the mosaic sculpture are dedicated to the memory of John Lennon, the famous musician and Beatles star that lived around the corner. The word "Imagine" honors the title of his famous song.

In Case You Wonder: Twenty-five million people visit Central Park every year!

Boy + Metal = Art

Rey David Rojas has been curious about art and metals all his life. It all started at the local blacksmith shop owned by his family outside Mexico City, where he would spend hours and hours bending, twisting, straightening, fastening, cutting, painting, and hammering all kind of metals. He would use wires, paper clips, screws, and nails and glue them together. He would also attach them to cardboard or pieces of wood to make sculptures.

Soon, play became a serious game for Rey David, who grew up to be a very good student and finished art school with honors.

Wire? Really?

Actually, the wire that Rey David uses is made with copper and covered with plastic. To begin, he carefully takes the plastic off the wire and makes a long roll with it. Using a photograph or a drawing of the shape he wants to make as a guide, he starts modeling the wire. This is very tricky. Rey David has to tie little knots and bend the wire many times. He doesn't really know how the sculpture is going to look until it is finished. Sometimes, it doesn't work and he has to start over. Rey David is very persistent, and he does the same sculpture over and over until he is happy with the result. When this happens, the piece is ready for its picture!

Click!

Rey David takes several photographs of each piece he does and puts them in his computer. Using special programs, he separates the wire structures from their backgrounds and puts finishing touches on the pieces. Then he adds his favorite colors as backgrounds.

Book Facts:

• The "Imagine" mosaic in Central Park was the hardest piece to make. Those little tiles took a long time!

• The paperclip is the smallest piece in this book. To make it, Rey David used 8 inches of wire, but the paperclip is only 1.9 inches long.

• The Statue of Liberty is big in real life and also in this book. It took almost 33 feet of wire to build the illustration, and the final piece measures 39 inches tall.

• 419 feet of wire were used in the making of this book.

• A small piece (like a bagel) takes 2 to 3 hours to make. Large pieces, such as the Brooklyn Bridge, may take 3 days to finish!

Rey David's Materials

• Copper wire

• Assorted pliers

• Hammer

• Welding gun

• Computer

• His imagination

• Two hands

! Safety First!

Creating things can be lots of fun, but it can also be dangerous. Metals are sharp and can hurt you. You can create sculptures like the ones in this book using pipe cleaners or other materials available at arts & crafts stores.

Rey David Rojas is an award-wining visual artist who studied in the renowned Escuela Nacional de Artes Plásticas (National School of Visual Arts) in Mexico City. Rey David works in a variety of mediums, including painting, photography and small-scale wire sculpture, and his work has been exhibited in Mexico and Spain. Rey David has illustrated children's books for some of Mexico's most innovative publishers, such as Editorial Serpentina and Editorial Escarabajo. He lives with his wife and children outside Mexico City.

Puck is the author of the series Cool Counting Books™ that includes **123 New York**, **123 USA**, **123 California**, **123 Chicago**, **123 Texas**, **123 San Francisco**, and **123 Philadelphia**. Puck lives in New York where one afternoon he crossed the Brooklyn Bridge with his wife and twin sons. While looking at the immense mesh of wire over him, he imagined a city made of wire. That idea became this book.

Library of Congress Control Number: 2009935647

ISBN: 978-0-9825295-0-8
Library Binding

Book design by Tahara Anderson

Published in 2010 by Duo Press, LLC

First Edition

Manufactured by CT Printing
Great Industrial Park, Shenzhen, China, 51811
September 2009